PUFFIN

STRANGER DANGER?

Joe learns his safety rules all right, but almost at once he gets confused. Things just aren't as easy as the policeman who came to school tries to make out. Why does his teacher send him out of class with a lady he's never even met before? Shouldn't he reply politely when strangers are friendly? Joe has an extraordinary day trying to get things right. There's one amusing blunder after another as, slowly but surely, Joe comes to learn that, even with the most important rules of all, you do still have to think!

Anne Fine was born and educated in the Midlands and now lives in Edinburgh with her two daughters and an assortment of pets. She has written numerous highly acclaimed and prize-winning books for children and teenagers. Her novel *Goggle-Eyes* won the *Guardian* Children's Fiction Award and the Carnegie Medal, and her book *Bill's New Frock* won the Smarties Prize.

For Sara Macaulay

Chapter One

On Monday morning a policeman came to Joe's class to show everybody a film and give them a talk.

The film was called *Stranger Danger*. Joe didn't see much of it. He was under the table, trying to coax a baby daddy-long-legs on to the palm

I

of his hand. He heard a bit of the film, though. He heard, *Never take sweets from a stranger*, and, *Never go with a stranger*. Joe thought the baby daddy-long-legs must have seen the same film. It wouldn't put even one step on Joe's hand, and Joe didn't like to pick it up in case one of its legs fell off.

Afterwards, the policeman spoke to everybody. He was good fun, and made a lot of jokes. Mostly he talked about being careful.

"Don't worry about being *too* careful," he said. "You *can't* be too careful. You have to use your common sense. Now, let's hear from everybody. What is the first safety rule?"

"Never take sweets from a stranger!" everyone chanted.

"Right!" said the policeman. "And that means food and drink and anything at all that goes in your mouth."

3

He paused, and stuck his thumb in his mouth like a baby. Everyone giggled.

He took his thumb out and looked serious again.

"And what is the other safety rule?" he asked.

"Never go with a stranger," everyone chanted.

"I can't hear you," he said, cupping his ears and looking puzzled.

"*Never go with a stranger*!" everyone shouted.

"I still can't hear," he said. "You'll have to speak up. I must be going a bit deaf."

"NEVER GO WITH A STRANGER," everyone bellowed.

"That's good," he said. "Now
don't forget!"

And winking goodbye at Joe's
teacher, Mrs Murray, he settled his
helmet back on his head, and went
off.

Joe looked down at the floor again, but, frightened by the noise, his baby daddy-long-legs had disappeared.

Chapter Two

Later, the classroom door swung
open and in walked a lady Joe had
never seen before. Steel spectacles
hung on a chain around her neck,
and in her hand she was carrying a
list.

"Eye tests," she said, and nodded
at Mrs Murray, who was busy in the
reading corner.

Mrs Murray nodded back.

The lady put on her spectacles and looked down her list. Joe hoped it wasn't in alphabetical order. He always came first.

"Arnold," she said. "Joe Arnold. Is he here?"

Joe put his head down and kept quiet.

Mrs Murray looked up from the reading corner and said, "Off you go, Joe."

Joe stared. The lady was a perfect stranger! Maybe she'd nodded across the room to Mrs Murray, but Joe had never seen her before in his life. And *Stranger Danger*. Hadn't the policeman only just finished showing them the film?

The lady was beginning to look
just a little bit impatient. She tapped
her list.

"Where are you, Joe?" she said. "Out you come."

Joe scraped his feet against the legs of his table, but he didn't stand up.

"Hurry up, Joe," said Mrs Murray. "It's only an eye test. You

just look at pictures and colours, and answer questions about what you see. Then we know if you need to wear glasses."

Still Joe didn't move. He sat fiddling with the pencils on his desk.

"Go along, Joe," said Mrs Murray. "Now!"

She sounded as if she meant it.

So Joe scraped back his chair and followed the lady out of the room. All the way down the corridor he was furious. He was angry with the lady, but he was even more angry with Mrs Murray. What was the point of inviting a policeman into the class to warn everybody *Never go with a stranger* when the first thing you did was get cross with someone who tried to do as they had been told?

He dragged his feet, falling even further behind.

The lady turned round.

"What *is* the matter with you, Joe?" she asked. "Are you nervous? Eye tests don't hurt."

Joe wanted to explain. "*Stranger Danger!*" he wanted to say. "I'm just trying to do what the policeman said." But, then again, the policeman also said you had to use your common sense. And they were still in the school corridor, with lots of people about. And if he yelled, they'd all come running straight away to see what was the matter. And the lady knew Mrs Murray,

and Mrs Murray knew her. And Joe
had taken a note home about the eye
tests. And the lady did have a real
alphabetical list with his full name
right at the top.

"All right," he said. And he
walked faster, to catch up.

The eye test was fun. He sat in
the chair, and she held a torch with
a tiny bright light that danced on his
eyeballs. She gave him a long tube
like a telescope to look through, and

held up odd shapes and fancy patterns that jumped before his eyes. Then she hung up a chart with some really silly pictures. There was a fish mending his socks under water, and an octopus pushing four prams at once. He enjoyed the eye test a lot, and was sorry when it finished.

"There," said the lady. "That wasn't so bad, was it?"

Joe grinned.

The lady studied her list.

"When you get back to your classroom," she said, "tell Simeon Barnes to run along and see me, will you?"

"Right," said Joe. And when he got back, he told Simeon he was next on the list.

Simeon just rushed off straight away.

Chapter Three

After school Joe ran home. It was a
special evening. Joe's brother Tom
had got his first important job
playing the violin in a big orchestra,
and all the family had tickets for the
concert even though it was miles
away, in Easthampton.

Nana was waiting at the door, all

dressed up in a new flowery suit. Joe
rushed upstairs. His mother was
crouched in front of the mirror in his
bedroom, wearing her fanciest dress
and putting on lipstick.

Joe looked at the clothes she'd
laid out for him on the bed. Last

year's smart trousers which were too tight now; his new white shirt that was too big still; old-fashioned shiny black shoes that used to belong to his brother; and the red tie he hated.

"I can't wear this lot."

Joe's mother smacked her lipsticky lips, and turned around.

"Joe," she said. "It's a very special evening. You think you'll look silly in these clothes, but when you get to the concert hall, you'll see you look like everybody else."

Joe didn't believe her, but he didn't bother to argue. Nobody ever won a battle with Mum when she was all dressed up and wearing lipstick.

Grandpa and Joe's father were

waiting by the car. They were in
dark suits and white shirts, too.
Even the car had been through the
car wash. It was, Joe realised, a very
special evening indeed.

It was a long journey. If anyone
had asked Joe what he'd done in

school, he might have told them about the policeman and the baby daddy-long-legs, and *Stranger Danger* and the safety rules. But they were all too busy talking about Tom and his violin, so in the end Joe fell asleep.

He only woke after they reached the concert hall. Joe stood with his grandparents on the wide marble steps, waiting for his parents to come back from parking the car. When they appeared, the two of them were strolling arm in arm, not looking like themselves at all, more like two smart and elegant guests in someone else's wedding photographs.

Then everyone walked up the

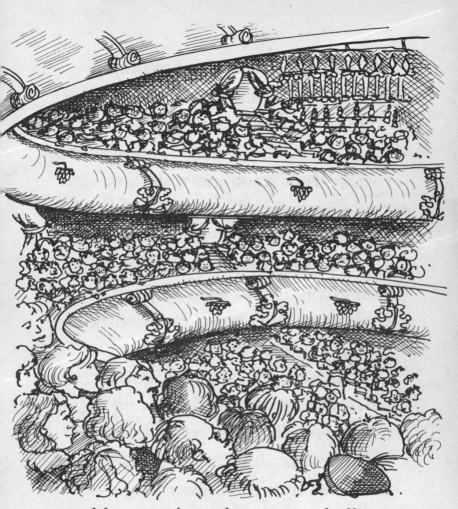

marble steps into the concert hall.
It was enormous. It was *massive*.
You could have driven buses

between the pillars in the corridors,
and that was just around the edges.

Inside, it was even more
astonishing – rows and rows of seats,
hundreds of rows, more than you
could have imagined in one
building. His whole school could
have sat in just two rows. You'd
practically need a rocket to get to
the ceiling. You could run half-mile
races round the edge.

Each seat was covered with red
velvet. Great chandeliers hung
overhead. Thick drapes held back
with golden ropes hung at each
doorway, and there were fifty
doorways at least. People were
milling through them, and everyone
was dressed smartly. A lot of the

men wore fancy bow-ties. Some of
the ladies' dresses brushed the floor.

"See?" Joe's mother said,
squeezing his arm. "It's a *very*
special evening."

Joe gazed up at the platform,
filled with empty chairs and music
stands.

"What about Tom?" he asked.
"Where will he sit?"

"Towards the back," said
Grandpa. "Third violins. It might
be just a little difficult to see him."

A little difficult? It was
impossible! When all the men and
women of the orchestra had filed in,
and bowed, and sat down to play
the first piece of music, all Joe could
see of his brother was the point of

his bow shooting up and down with all the other third violins at the back.

His mother didn't seem to mind, though. She sat on the very edge of her red velvet seat, and stared over the sea of grey curly perms and bald heads as if Tom were sitting right at the front.

And his father didn't seem to mind, either. He leaned back in his

seat and closed his eyes, and smiled
as the music floated over him.

Nana also had her eyes closed.
But she wasn't smiling as the music
floated over her. She was asleep.
The seats were soft and comfortable,
and it had been a long drive.

Grandpa wasn't asleep, but he
wasn't listening to the music either.
He'd switched his hearing-aid off.

Joe watched him peeping furtively towards Nana to check that she was really asleep; then, stealthily, he slid the little plastic control box out of his pocket, and flicked the tiny lever from ON to OFF.

Joe couldn't blame him. The music was pretty boring. All swoopings and swirlings of violins, which was probably why his brother Tom was so keen on it. It didn't seem to *go* anywhere. It just went on and on and on. Joe settled down for a really boring time.

And then he felt a tickle in his throat.

Cough!

Joe looked round, panicking.

Cough, cough!

The tickle was worse.

Cough, cough, cough, cough!

The man in front shifted irritably in his seat. The noise was bothering him, you could tell.

Cough, cough, cough, *cough*!

The lady on Joe's left was glowering at him now. He wondered

if he ought to squeeze past her, and all the other people between himself and the gangway, and leave the concert hall. But when he glanced round, all he could see was the long, long walk up the aisle to the doorway, and thousands of people who would stare at him.

Cough, *cough*, cough, *cough*!

His cheeks were fiery with embarrassment. In his ears, his coughing sounded louder than the music. He longed to crouch down in his seat, roll up and disappear – *anything*. His cough was ruining this very special evening.

Suddenly he felt a tap on his shoulder. Oh, no! Someone had had enough! Terrified, he twisted in his

seat and turned to face whoever was
going to complain. But he was
wrong. It wasn't a scowling face at
all. It was a white-haired gentleman
who was leaning forward and
offering him a peppermint to suck.

Gratefully Joe reached out – then
remembered the other safety rule:

Never take sweets from a stranger. He
drew his hand back smartly, as if
he'd been scorched, and shook his

head. He thought the old gentleman might be irritated with him for changing his mind at the last moment. But he just shrugged and looked sorry for Joe, as if he understood why he couldn't take one.

But sorry doesn't help.

Cough, *cough, cough, cough*!

Joe was in misery. He turned to his parents, but Mum was still gazing enraptured towards the orchestra, and Dad was still leaning back with his eyes closed. How could he ask if it was all right to take a peppermint? He couldn't reach far enough to jog Dad's elbow. He couldn't whisper to Grandpa to do it because the hearing-aid was

switched off. And if he woke Nana
suddenly, she'd shoot upright and
yell, "*What*?" very loudly. She
always did. It came from living with
Grandpa who was always switching
off his hearing-aid.

Cough, cough, cough, cough!

And all he needed was a
peppermint!

Cough, *cough*!

"You have to use your common sense," the policeman had said. Joe thought about it. Here he was, safe in a huge concert hall filled with people. The old gentleman offered him the peppermint because he couldn't stop coughing. He wasn't trying to poison him. And if Joe only could have asked, he knew his mother would have smiled her thanks at the old gentleman, and let him take it.

Joe swivelled in his seat and gave the man a pleading look. Luckily he understood at once, and leaning forward in his seat, he offered the peppermints again.

Joe took one and popped it in his mouth. The cough stopped at once.

The man in front stopped shifting
in his seat. The lady on his left
stopped glowering. Even the music
began to sound soothing. Joe felt so
relieved, he almost found himself
enjoying the swooping, swirling
violins.

Minutes passed, but the cough
never returned to bother him. He
spent the time pleasantly enough.

He counted bald heads bobbing up and down in front of him. And then grey perms. But, mostly, he just sat listening to the music and thinking of the lady who swept him off for the eye test and the old gentleman who gave him the peppermint.

Most strangers are probably good people, Joe thought. And it's nice to be friendly. If someone you've never seen before says, "New bike?" to you on the pavement, you like to be able to tell them, "Yes, it's my birthday present." And when you're patting a puppy outside a shop and then the owner comes out and says, "It's all right. He won't bite", it's nice to ask, "How old is he?" or "What's his name?" You don't just shrug and set your face and walk away. You try to be pleasant.

But you have to stay safe, too. That's why they make you learn the safety rules – so you will always stop and think, and always use your common sense.

Then, while Joe was still thinking about it, the violins seemed to gather themselves up for the very last time, and with a tremendous drum roll and a clash of cymbals, the music finished. Nana shot upright and yelled "*What*?" but no one heard her over the outburst of applause. Seeing hands clapping all around him, Grandpa furtively slid his hand in his pocket to switch his hearing-aid back from OFF to ON.

And when the orchestra stood up to take a bow, Joe even saw his brother Tom lift his head quicker than any of the others, and give a quick wink over their bent backs.

The concert was over.

Chapter Four

After the clapping ended, the orchestra filed off the stage, and everyone in the hall began to shuffle towards the doorways, politely saying, "Excuse me" and "I beg your pardon" as they trampled on one another's toes.

Joe's father glanced at Nana,

whose eyelids were still droopy from sleep.

"You stay here while we fetch the car," he said.

"Stay close to Nana and Grandpa, Joe," Mum warned. "Don't disappear in the crowd."

They hurried ahead to the car park while Nana and Grandpa took their time, waiting for the crush to thin a little before they tried to get through the doorway. Outside, the marble steps were wet, and there were puddles everywhere. People were vanishing into the darkness.

Joe stood beneath an archway and watched as Nana and Grandpa helped one another slowly and carefully down the first few steps.

Suddenly a man slipped through the
archway beside Joe. He wore a
musician's dark suit and white bow
tie, and he was carrying a black
case, taller and fatter than himself,

and shaped like a vast overgrown violin. Joe knew enough about an orchestra to guess there was a double bass inside. He watched with interest. Maybe this man was a friend of his brother's.

Just as the man hurried by, Joe heard a sudden *snap*. The lock on the double bass case had broken. Almost at once, the wide stiff front began to swing open.

Hastily the man threw his arms around it to push it shut. Then he rested the case on the ground and thought for a moment. Joe saw the problem straight away. If the man started down the marble steps, the lid would swing open again. His double bass might tumble out, and

clatter down the steps and be
ruined.

The man was frowning now. He
looked at his watch. Then he
glanced up and saw Joe standing,
watching.

The man's face cleared.

"Hello there!" he called out in a friendly way. "Could you give me a little bit of help here? Can you help me carry this down to the car park?"

Joe glanced down the steps. Nana and Grandpa were almost at the bottom now. They would be turning to look for him in a moment.

He could say yes. The man had asked for help. And he was in the orchestra. And he might even be a friend of Tom's . . .

But Joe could say no, too. And though there were still lots of people

on the steps, he wasn't so sure about
bits of the car park. He ought to stay
close to Nana and Grandpa. It
might seem mean, or even rude. But
there was the safety rule, after all.
Never go with a stranger.

Joe shook his head and started
down the steps.

"I'm sorry," he called back. "I have to stay close."

And without waiting to hear whether the man replied or not, he scampered towards Nana and Grandpa as fast as possible.

Grandpa was holding Nana by the arm, and peering at headlights, trying to see if the right car was coming.

Joe took his hand. "A man asked me to help him carry a case to the car park," he said. "But I told him I had to stay close to you."

"Good lad," said Grandpa. "Better safe than sorry."

"I felt a bit mean," Joe said. "He looked a nice man, and he really needed help."

Grandpa was still peering into
oncoming headlights. "You still did
the right thing," he said. "If he
needs help, he'll find it. Don't you
worry."

Joe bit his lip. "He won't think
I'm rude?"

But Grandpa had spotted the car now, and he was busy waving it to a halt. So Nana answered.

"No," she said firmly. "He won't think you're rude. Good strangers always understand that you're just doing what you're told to do to stay safe. That's the good thing about safety rules. They make it easy to say no."

The car door was open now. As Nana clambered in, Joe thought about what she'd said. She was right. That *was* the good thing about safety rules. First they reminded you to stop and think and use your common sense. Then they made it easy to say no. And good strangers always understood.

"Good," he said. "*Good*."

Just as he was about to climb into
the car, a strong arm slid from
nowhere around his waist, and
hauled him back.

"What's good?" a gruff voice sounded in his ear. "The concert hall? The music? Or those very, very special third violins?"

Joe swung around. Stranger danger?

No. No one strange at all. Just his brother Tom in his dark suit and white bow tie, standing beside him clutching his violin case, and looking very, very proud.

Some other Young Puffins

ANOTHER BIG STORY BOOK
ed. Richard Bamberger

One of the foremost experts on literature for children has col-
lected here some of the world's most enchanting and magical
fairy tales. From the English tale 'Jack and the Beanstalk' to
the Indian 'Wali Dad the Simple', these are stories parents
will enjoy telling and children will remember with pleasure
for the rest of their lives.

BAD BOYS
ed. Eileen Colwell

All the boys in these twelve stories are bad in one way or
another. Either really bad, like Freddie, Adolphus, Edward,
Montague, Montmorency and John Henry, who leave their
aunts marooned on an island, or only a little bad, like
Timothy, who jumps in and out of puddles.

THE PARENTS BOOK OF
BEDTIME STORIES
Edited by Tony Bradman

Bedtime will always be a pleasure with this refreshing book of
bedtime stories drawn from the popular Parents magazine.
With plenty of lively and appealing characters and a wide
range of themes (and all the perfect length for a bedtime slot),
this is an ideal addition to the family bookshelf.

ENOUGH IS ENOUGH
Margaret Nash

Usually when Miss Boswell uses her magic phrase, it works:
Class 1 know that she means enough is *enough*, and get back to
work, for a while at least. But when Miss Boswell's special
plant begins to grow and grow until it has wiped the sums off
the board, curled right out of the classroom and is heading for
the kitchen, not even shouting 'Enough is enough' will stop it!

HELP!
Margaret Gordon

Fred and Flo are very helpful little pigs. The problem is, the
more helpful they try to be, the more trouble they cause.
Whether they are washing Grandad's car, looking after Baby
or doing the decorating, disaster is never far away! Four
hilarious stories featuring two very charming – and helpful –
piglets.

KING KEITH AND THE NASTY
CASE OF DRAGONITUS
Kaye Umansky

When cowardly King Keith goes down with a right royal
cold, he refuses to take his horrid medicine. So how can he
possibly persuade a tearful, spotty dragon with the dreaded
Dragonitus to be brave and take *his* nasty medicine?

And in the second story, King Keith is in a right royal sulk.
His show-off cousin King Clive has invited himself to tea.
They never liked each other before – will they be able to settle
old scores?

DUSTBIN CHARLIE
Ann Pilling

Charlie has always liked seeing what people threw out in their dustbins. So he's thrilled to find the toy of his dreams among the rubbish in the skip. But during the night, someone else takes it. The culprit in this highly enjoyable story turns out to be the most surprising person.

CLASS THREE AND THE BEANSTALK
Martin Waddell

Two unusual stories which will amaze you. Class Three's project of growing things gets out of hand after they plant a packet of Jackson's Giant Bean seeds. And when Wilbur Small is coming home, the whole street is buzzing – except for Tom Grice and his family, who are new in the street so don't know what the fuss is about, or why people are so nervous!

THE TWIG THING
Jan Mark

As soon as Rosie and Ella saw the house they knew that something was missing. It had lots of windows and stairs, but where was the garden? When they move in, they find a twig thing which they put in water on the window-sill, and gradually things begin to change.

NO HOLIDAY FUN FOR SAM

Thelma Lambert

When Sam sees the words NO BUCKETS AND SPADES in his hotel, he knows he's in for a dismal holiday. Kippers for breakfast and pouring rain . . . will he ever survive it? Added to that, Sam's cub pack plan to go camping in Wales and Sam is really excited at the idea, but well-laid plans can go wrong . . .

THE GREMLIN BUSTER

Rosemary Hayes

Peter doesn't know what a gremlin is but he does know that there's something very strange going on. He creeps down to the kitchen in the middle of the night and finds a green, nasty and very angry creature right inside the washing machine. It *is* a gremlin, but it's far too clever to be caught and soon it's in the cooker, the vacuum cleaner and even the TV. What can Peter do to stop it?

ZOT'S TREASURES

Ivan Jones

What has Zot the dog found this time? Is it a hat, or a monster? Some delicious jelly, or just an old bone? Bouncy Zot and his friend Clive go looking for buried treasure and have all sorts of funny adventures in these five jolly stories.

ANNE FINE

STRANGER DANGER?

Illustrated by Jean Baylis

PUFFIN BOOKS

PUFFIN BOOKS

Published by the Penguin Group
Penguine Books Ltd, 27 Wrights Lane, London w8 5tz, England
Penguine Books USA Inc., 375 Hudson Street, New York, New York 10014, USA
Penguin Books Australia Ltd, Ringwood, Victoria, Australia
Penguin Books Canada Ltd, 2801 John Street, Markham, Ontario, Canada l3r 1b4
Penguin Books (NZ) Ltd, 182–190 Wairau Road, Auckland 10, New Zealand

Penguin Books Ltd, Registered Offices: Harmondsworth, Middlesex, England

First published by Hamish Hamilton Children's Books 1989
Published in Puffin Books 1991
1 3 5 7 9 10 8 6 4 2

Filmset in Baskerville (Linotron 202) by
CentraCet, Cambridge
Printed in England by Clays Ltd, St Ives plc